# the Tweeting Cat

Tweets by
Ollie Fallon Gervais
Illustrated
by Rich Nairn

£1 from every Tweeting Cat book sold will be donated to the
Celia Hammond Animal Trust on behalf of #OllieAid.
www.celiahammond.org

## INTRODUCTION
## BY HRH
## OLLIE FALLON GERVAIS

GREETINGS, ADORING FANS!!

AS MANY OF YOU KNOW, I LOVE TO TWEET. MOSTLY ABOUT HOW BRILLIANT I AM AND MY TIRELESS WORK BEING A PHILANTHROPIST, SUPERMODEL, PERSONAL TRAINER CAT AND ALL ROUND BUSY BUSINESSCAT. SOMETIMES ABOUT OTHER IMPORTANT STUFF TOO, LIKE MY 91 (AT THE TIME OF PUBLICATION) FIANCÉS, IF I GOT MY DINNER ON TIME, OR IF MY MUM AND DAD HAVE GONE AWAY AND LEFT 'THE IDIOTS' IN CHARGE OF ME. ONCE I TWEETED ABOUT HOW I MAY OR MAY NOT HAVE DONE A WEE ON MY MUM AND DAD'S BED WHEN THEY WEREN'T LOOKING, BUT WE DON'T TALK ABOUT THAT.

WHEN MR RICH NAIRN APPROACHED ME AND ASKED IF HE COULD DO A BOOK OF HIS BRILLIANT ILLUSTRATIONS OF SOME OF MY TWEETS, - AND RAISE SOME MONEY FOR SAD CATS AT THE SAME TIME - OF COURSE I SAID 'YES' BECAUSE I AM A WELL-KNOWN PHILANTHROPIST (DID I ALREADY MENTION THAT?) AND I LOVE TO HELP SAD ANIMALS THROUGH MY GROUNDBREAKING INITIATIVE 'OLLIE AID'. ALSO IT WAS FRANKLY ABOUT TIME SOMEONE DID A BOOK ABOUT ME (IN YOUR FACE STREETCAT BOB, THAT'LL TEACH YOU NOT TO REPLY TO MY TWEETS. LET'S SEE WHO GETS A FILM MADE ABOUT THEM NOW, SHALL WE?)

**Ollie** @myleftfang

MY MUM & DAD HAVE POPPED OUT
TO GET ME SOME HAMSTER JAM!!!

RICH NAIRN '18

**Ollie** @myleftfang

THERE IS NO SUCH THING AS
HAMSTER JAM!! I'VE BEEN CONNED!!

RICH NAIRN '18

**Ollie** @myleftfang

DEAR IDIOTS, I AM SITTING ON THIS THRONE BECAUSE
I AM QUEEN OF THE HOUSE. YOU ARE A PAIR OF LOWLY
BASTARDS WHO ARE NOT WORTHY OF SHARING THE
SAME SPACE AS ME. NOW GIMME MY LUNCH.

RICH NAIRN '18

 **Ollie** @myleftfang

SOMETIMES I AM IN AWE OF THE BEAUTY OF THIS
WORLD. MOST OF THE TIME I'M JUST LOOKING IN THE
MIRROR IN AWE OF THE BEAUTY OF ME.
#PhilosopherCat

RICH NAIRN '18

**Ollie** @myleftfang

SUNDAY SNOOZING IN THE SUN!!
#Snoozin

RICH NAIRN '18

**Ollie** @myleftfang

I DON'T UNDERSTAND PEOPLE SAYING MY
FEETIES AREN'T DAINTY! LOOK AT THEM!!
THEY'RE THE DEFINITION OF LADYLIKE!!
#Haters

RICH NAIRN '18

**Ollie** @myleftfang

ME? BRAG? AS IF! JUST BECAUSE I WAS ON PRIME
TIME NATIONAL TV THIS MORNING & AM NOW THE
MOST FAMOUSEST, BELOVED, BEAUTIFUL, SMART
CAT IN THE WORLD??

RICH NAIRN '18

 **Ollie** @myleftfang

MY MUM JUST GAVE THE FOX A TIN OF POSH CAT
FOOD THAT SOMEONE SENT FOR ME!!! I'M THE POSH
CAT ROUND HERE!! SHE SAYS I CAN'T HAVE IT
BECAUSE OF MY SENSITIVE TUMMY. WHAT IF FOXY
HAS A SENSITIVE TUMMY, MUMMY??? YOU DIDN'T
THINK OF THAT, DID YOU?? GIMME!!
#NotFair

**Ollie** @myleftfang

IT ALL LOOKS VERY STRANGE OUT THERE.
#Brrrrr

RICH NAIRN '18

**Ollie** @myleftfang

HELLO! IS THAT THE POLICE??? IT'S TOO COLD IN
MY HOUSE!!! DO SOMETHING ABOUT IT!!!

RICH NAIRN '18

**Ollie** @myleftfang

I'M HAVING A SNOW DAY!!
#StayingIn #Snoozing

**Ollie** @myleftfang

WHERE'S MY LUNCH?? IT'S THREE MINUTES
PAST ONE!!! POLICE!!

**Ollie** @myleftfang

GET AWAY FROM ME!! I INTEND TO SLEEP FROM NOW UNTIL MY MUM AND DAD GET BACK!!!

 **Ollie** @myleftfang

IT'S MONDAY PEOPLES!! IT'S COLD & WET & I CAN'T BE BOTHERED TO DO ANY WORK. GOING BACK TO BED. #WheresMyMum

**Ollie** @myleftfang

I WAS REALLY LOOKING FORWARD TO LETTING MY MUM BRUSH ME ALL DAY FOR MOTHER'S DAY, BUT WHY ARE THE IDIOTS HERE?????

**Ollie** @myleftfang

STILL TAKING MY SUNDAY SNOOZING VERY SERIOUSLY #Snoozin

**Ollie** @myleftfang

I AM NOT A BIG FAT HAIRY MOUSE FACED SPIKEY THING!!

RICH NAIRN '18

**Ollie** @myleftfang

I WAS PRACTICING MY WELCOME HOME SONG FOR MY MUM & DAD, BUT THE IDIOTS TOOK AWAY MY PIANO, BECAUSE THEY SAID I WAS MAKING TOO MUCH NOISE!!

RICH NAIRN '18

**Ollie** @myleftfang

THIS IS HOW MY BRILLIANT SONG WAS GOING TO GO: MUMMY I LOVE YOOOOOO, DADDY I LOVE YOOOOOOOU, WHERE HAVE YOU BEEEEN? DON'T EVER GO AWAY AGAAAAIN! HOW DARE YOU LEAVE ME WITH THOSE BASTAAAAARDS!!! I'M CALLING THE POLIIIIICE!!!

RICH NAIRN '18

**Ollie** @myleftfang

LOOK EVERYONE I'M TWITTER FAMOUS!! AND IT'S NOT TRUE MY MUM RUNS MY ACCOUNT. IT'S JUST WHEN I TWEET THINGS ABOUT HOW BRILLIANT & BEAUTIFUL I AM, THAT'S HER. AS YOU ALL KNOW, I AM WAY TOO HUMBLE TO DO THAT!

RICH NAIRN '18

**Ollie** @myleftfang

I'VE BEEN TELLING MY MUM & DAD EVERYTHING THAT'S HAPPENED IN THE PAST WEEK FOR MANY HOURS NOW, AND I'M NOT EVEN HALFWAY THROUGH!!

RICH NAIRN '18

 **Ollie** @myleftfang

I'M BEING MADE TO WORK ON A SATURDAY!! SATURDAYS ARE FOR SNOOZING!!
#WriteYourOwnSitcomDad
#WheresMyWagesAt

RICH NAIRN '18

**Ollie** @myleftfang

MY MUM'S YOGA CLASS
IS ABOUT TO START.
I WILL BE SUPERVISING!!
#PersonalTrainerCat

**Ollie** @myleftfang

HAVE MY UNIFORM READY!! THIS
#PERSONALTRAINERCAT IS DOING OVERTIME
TOMORROW!!

**Ollie** @myleftfang

HIT THAT THING HARDER!!
#PersonalTrainerBoxingCat #Roboleg

**Ollie** @myleftfang

IT MIGHT BE A BANK HOLIDAY BUT IT'S ALL WORK
WORK WORK FOR THIS DEDICATED NURSEY!
#NurseOllie #Roboleg

**Ollie** @myleftfang

DO I SNORE SOMETIMES??? SO WHAT???
ALL THE MOST LADYLIKE LADIES DO!!!

**Ollie** @myleftfang

MR HOOVER HAS COME ROUND!!
SOMEONE CALL THE POLICE!!!!!!

**Ollie** @myleftfang

I'VE DECIDED TO
FORM A UNION!!
THE BUSYBUSINESSCAT,
NURSEY PHILANTHROPIST,
PERSONAL TRAINER
COMEDIAN SUPERMODEL
UNION! SO FAR IT HAS
ONE MEMBER (ME)!

RICH NAIRN '18

 **Ollie** @myleftfang

IT'S A BEAUTIFUL DAY!! THE GARDEN IS FULL OF
BIRDIES & SQUIRRELS THAT I CAN WATCH FROM
THE WINDOW!! BUT FIRST I NEED TO STUDY THIS
CUSHION. IT'S FASCINATING.

**Ollie** @myleftfang

🎵🎵 IT'S FRIDAY!! I'M SITTING IN MY BOX!! IT'S THE WEEEEKEND!! I'M HAVING SOME TIME OFF!!!! *
*No time off currently scheduled
#NurseOllie

**Ollie** @myleftfang

SATURDAY. SUNBATHING.
#SaturdaySunbathing #AndSnoozing #MainlySnoozing

**Ollie** @myleftfang
I'VE GOT MYSELF
A FEW BOOKS TO
READ SO I DON'T
HAVE TO TALK TO
THE IDIOTS
#LiteraryCat

**Ollie** @myleftfang

SOME PEOPLE HAVE ASKED TO SEE MY DIPLOMA
FROM THE NURSEYVERSITY (WHO ARE YOU,
DONALD TRUMP??) SO HERE IT IS!
#BestNurseyEver

Ollie @myleftfang

Ollie @myleftfang

PERSONAL TRAINER CAT
IS BACK IN BUSINESS!!!
#PTCat

Ollie @myleftfang

I LIKE TO HELP MY MUM STRETCH
AFTER A WORKOUT!!
#PersonalTrainerCat

**Ollie** @myleftfang

HAPPY FATHER'S DAY, MY DAD!!! FOR YOUR PRESENT, I THOUGHT YOU COULD GIVE ME MY BREAKFAST (S) INSTEAD OF MUM & THEN BRUSH ME BEFORE WE SNUGGLE!!!

**Ollie** @myleftfang

REMEMBER WHEN IT WAS BRING YOUR DAUGHTER TO WORK DAY?
#HappyFathersDayMyDad

MY DAD STARTED FILMING HIS NEW SERIES TODAY
& I JUST FOUND OUT IT HAS A D.O.G. IN IT!!!!
GET AWAY FROM MY DAD YOU BASTARD!!!!

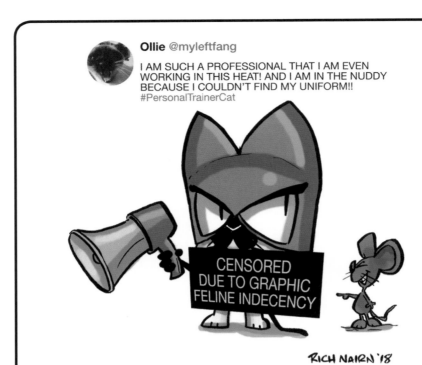

**Ollie** @myleftfang

TOO HOT TO TWEET

**Ollie** @myleftfang

I CAN'T BELIEVE I'VE HAD TO WORK ON MY BIRTHDAY!!! SO I MADE SURE I WORE HER OUT!!
#PersonalTrainerCat

**Ollie** @myleftfang

I JUST GOT TAKEN TO THE V.E.T!!!
THE DAY AFTER MY BIRTHDAY!!!
TURNS OUT I HAVE A BIT OF
ARTHUR-ITUS, WHICH I MUST
HAVE CAUGHT FROM MY FIANCÉ
ARTHUR!!
THE V.E.T DID SAY MY LOVELY
COAT MAKES ME LOOK MORE
LIKE 3 THAN 15, THOUGH!

**Ollie** @myleftfang

ME & MY FABULOUS TOOTSIES ARE GOING TO
SPEND THE DAY LYING IN THE PATH OF MY NEW
FRIEND THE FAN!! #TootsieTuesday

**Ollie** @myleftfang

I'M SNOOZIN ON ME THRONE DON'CHA KNOW
#Snootingdon

RICH NAIRN '18

**Ollie** @myleftfang

ME AND MY MUM ARE WORKING AT THE KITCHEN TABLE!! #BusyBusinessCat #Muse

RICH NAIRN '18

RICH NAIRN '18

RICH NAIRN '18

**Ollie** @myleftfang
PT SESSION WITH MY MUM!!
#PersonalTrainerCat

**Ollie** @myleftfang
HOLD THAT WEIGHT!!!
DON'T DROP IT!!! I SAID
DON'T DROP IT!!! I DON'T
CARE IF IT'S HEAVY!!!!!
#PersonalTrainerCat
#IWantDangerMoney

**Ollie** @myleftfang

STEP ON THE BOX, STEP OFF THE BOX,
STEP ON THE BOX, STEP OFF THE BOX,
STEP ... OH FOR GODSSAKE
MAKE UP YOUR MIND,
IT'S TOO EARLY
FOR THIS!!!
#PersonalTrainerCat

**Ollie** @myleftfang

I WAS BEING #PersonalTrainerCat TODAY!
THIS IS ME LETTING MY MUM KNOW I'M
FURIOUS THAT SHE WON'T DO 5 MORE
MINUTES!!

**Ollie** @myleftfang

SATURDAY. SNOOZIN. WHERE'S MY FRIKKEN
BREAKFAST???
#SaturdaySnoozing #Gimme

**Ollie** @myleftfang

MY MUM!! IT'S TIME FOR OUR REGULAR PT
SESSION!! WHERE ARE YOU??? I'VE BEEN
WAITING AGES!!!!
#NoUniformNecessaryIfSheDoesntShowUp
#PersonalTrainerCat

**Ollie** @myleftfang

I WATCHED THE OMEN LAST NIGHT & THEN
THIS HAPPENED! AAAAAGH!!!!

 **Ollie** @myleftfang

I THINK THIS IS GOING
TO BE THE COVER FOR
MY NEW ALBUM,
'CAT OUT OF HELL'!!!

**Ollie** @myleftfang
THAT ANKLE STILL LOOKS WEIRD TO ME.
JUST SAYING.
#PersonalTrainerCat

**Ollie** @myleftfang
YOU'D TELL ME IF THERE WAS
SOMETHING BEHIND ME, RIGHT?

**Ollie** @myleftfang

MY MUM & DAD HAD LOTS OF PEOPLE OVER
LAST NIGHT & THEY SHUT ME IN A ROOM
UPSTAIRS WITH ALL MY STUFF SO I 'DIDN'T
GET TRODDEN ON'!!!!
THERE HAD BETTER BE LOTS OF THINGS
IN THIS NEXT WEEK, JUST SAYING #CatAbuse

**Ollie** @myleftfang

THEY DIDN'T LET ME OUT
TILL ABOUT 2 IN THE
MORNING, WHEN THERE
WERE ONLY A FEW PEOPLE
LEFT. I WENT DOWNSTAIRS,
SHOUTED AT THEM ALL
A COUPLE OF TIMES
& WENT STRAIGHT BACK
UP! THAT SHOWED THEM!!

**Ollie** @myleftfang

SO JUST TO BE CLEAR, THERE IS NO ONE
COMING ROUND TONIGHT SO YOU'RE NOT
GOING TO SHUT ME IN A ROOM AGAIN.
I HAVE HAD A SHORT CONTRACT DRAWN UP.
SIGN HERE #PoliceOnSpeedDial

 **Ollie** @myleftfang

OK LET'S GET THIS PARTY STARTED!
WHO WANTS A WHISKEY???

**StanTheMouse** @MouseStan

Managed to escape HRH @myleftfang long enough to do my first tweet.. there, done.

RICH NAIRN '19

**StanTheMouse** @MouseStan

Finally have a platform where I can highlight the important issues facing the world today! #endmouseslavery

RICH NAIRN '19

**StanTheMouse** @MouseStan

While HRH was being #personaltrainercat for the Queen Mum @janefallon last week, I went on a blind date. I'll be honest, I smelt a rat.

RICH NAIRN '19

**StanTheMouse** @MouseStan

It's Sunday, a day of rest. Therefore HRH has only set me a magazine size list of tasks to do today, not the usual 250 page book. #generousemployer

RICH NAIRN '19

**Ollie** @myleftfang

I'M DOING MY PROMO GIRL DUTIES LYING DOWN TODAY BECAUSE I'M A BIT UNDER THE WEATHER. BUY MY MUM'S NEW BOOK SO I CAN HAVE A DAY OFF!

**StanTheMouse** @MouseStan

Dr Stanley Cheeseman reporting for duty. Ready to give you your jabs Your Highness. @myleftfang

**Ollie** @myleftfang

NOW I'M PLAYING WITH
MY SPROUTY!!!

**StanTheMouse** @MouseStan

Job 248 for today.. Counselling session for
HRH's traumatised toy, Mr Sprouty.

**StanTheMouse** @MouseStan

Scones with cream and those little pots of jam
should really come with a warning to mice.

RICH NAIRN '19

 **StanTheMouse** @MouseStan

Rufus has joined me for lunch. He wouldn't fit
in the mouse hole so we're eating at the kitchen table.

RICH NAIRN '19

**StanTheMouse** @MouseStan

Found a couple of pics from a photoshoot I had a
few years back. Crazy days.

RICH NAIRN '19

 **StanTheMouse** @MouseStan

Another old photo. This one is from back in the days
when I was head of the Rat Pack. Fun times that involved
no crime whatsoever, despite the rumours.

RICH NAIRN '19

**Ollie** @myleftfang

MY NEW FUR IS GROWING BACK
ALL BROWNY!!!

RICH NAIRN '19

**Ollie** @myleftfang

I'VE JUST BEEN TO THE V.E.T TO HAVE MY CALCIUM
LEVELS CHECKED & THEY DIDN'T HAVE TO SEDATE
ME TO TAKE BLOOD!! I WAS A REALLY GOOD GIRL
& DIDN'T EVEN TRY TO BITE ANYONE! WAITING FOR
THE RESULTS.

RICH NAIRN '19

**Ollie** @myleftfang

I'M HAVING A STARE OFF
WITH MY DAD!

**Ollie** @myleftfang

SATURDAY. SNOOZIN. SOMEONE MAKE
ME A WOOLY JUMPER, I'M FREEZING!!
#SaturdaySnoozing

**StanTheMouse** @MouseStan

HRH might be impressive as #personaltrainercat
but two can play at the superhero game..
Meet THE AMAZING CHEESEBALL!!
#amazingcheeseball

RICH NAIRN '19

**StanTheMouse** @MouseStan

So my first mission as THE AMAZING
CHEESEBALL was to liberate some tuna..
turns out tuna are quite lazy and look
nothing like they do on the Discovery Channel.
#amazingcheeseball

RICH NAIRN '19

**StanTheMouse** @MouseStan

The AMAZING CHEESEBALL is back in action!
There's cheese trapped in the fridge that needs
rescuing!
#amazingcheeseball

**StanTheMouse** @MouseStan

Come Dine With Me is on. Disappointing.
Not enough cheese.

**StanTheMouse** @MouseStan

Suspect foul play. Phoning the police as Harry has been missing since going off to try on the lettuce negligee Ollie made him.

RICH NAIRN '19

**StanTheMouse** @MouseStan

Well this is embarrassing.. Harry just turned up. He'd got a job wearing the lettuce negligee Ollie made him in a mouse strip club down the corridor.

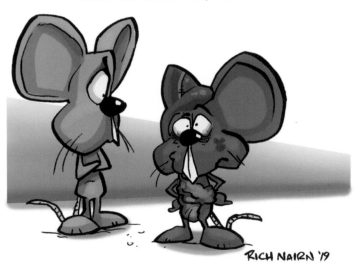

RICH NAIRN '19

**StanTheMouse** @MouseStan

I've got myself a pet that I've hidden in the garden. Don't suppose The Royal Mum & Dad will mind but HRH might just kill me.

RICH NAIRN '19

**StanTheMouse** @MouseStan

A bloody ant just turned up in the mouse hole claiming to be a travelling salesman.. time to call pest control.

RICH NAIRN '19

**Ollie** @myleftfang

WHERE'S MY DINNER???

**StanTheMouse** @MouseStan

Thought I'd make up for my lack of tweets with one really big one.

**StanTheMouse** @MouseStan

Right, who farted?!
I need my beauty sleep!

RICH NAIRN '19

**StanTheMouse** @MouseStan

Dear Diary, I'm getting this peculiar notion that all of my misfortunes are the invention of some demented cartoonist.

RICH NAIRN '19

Ollie @myleftfang

SMUSHIN!!!

# OLLIE'S BIOGRAPHY
## (I DIDN'T WRITE THIS BIT OBVIOUSLY - OLLIE)*

OLLIE FALLON GERVAIS WAS BORN IN JULY 2003. SHE IS RENOWNED FOR HER BEAUTY, HER CHARITY WORK, HER BRILLIANT JOKES, HER SKILLS AS A PERSONAL TRAINER CAT, AND IS FAMOUSLY THE WORLD'S BEST NURSEY, ESPECIALLY WHEN HER MUM HAD A LIMPY LEG (SHE ATTENDED THE NURSEYVERSITY). SHE HAD THE GREATEST EXTRA-LONG LEFT FANG EVER UNTIL IT WAS CRUELLY REMOVED IN 2016. HER FAVOURITE THINGS ARE: HER MUM AND DAD, HER BRUSHY, BLUE MOUSEY AND HER CATBERRY. HER LEAST FAVOURITE THINGS ARE THE IDIOTS, D.O.G.S AND V.E.T.S. SHE HAS THE POLICE ON SPEED DIAL. SHE IS PROBABLY THE BEST CAT IN THE WORLD.

*(Yes she did! - Stan the Mouse)

### *About the artist*

Rich Nairn is a cartoonist/caricaturist based in Kent, England, who also goes by the name of The Artful Doodler.

He has loved delving into the snapshots of Ollie's life that are the tweets of @myleftfang and creating these cartoons, while sniggering like a lunatic in his Doodle Cave.
See more by following Rich on Twitter @richnairn.

Rich also writes and illustrates the Dr Ripper & Co comedy horror books available on Amazon.

You can see many examples of his work by visiting his website at
www.theartfuldoodler.co.uk.

Printed in Great Britain
by Amazon

57097598R00046